TONY BALONEY

Yo Ho Ho, Halloween!

BY
PAM MUÑOZ RYAN

ILLUSTRATED BY
EDWIN FOTHERINGHAM

SCHOLASTIC PRESS • NEW YORK

To William Ryan Abel —P.M.R.

To my family —E.F.

LIBRARY OF CONGRESS CATALOGING-IN-PUBLICATION DATA AVAILABLE

ISBN 978-0-545-90885-6
10 9 8 7 6 5 4 3 2 1   16 17 18 19 20
Printed in China   62
First edition, July 2016

The text in this book was set in Adobe Caslon Pro Regular.
The display type was set in P22 Kane.
The title was hand lettered by Edwin Fotheringham.
The illustrations were created using digital media.
Book design by Marijka Kostiw

CONTENTS

Best Costume Ever

Halloween is coming!

Tony Baloney, the macaroni penguin, can't wait for the Halloween parade at school.

1. No costumes at school until the day of the parade.
2. Nothing pointy or dangerous at school, ever.
3. Use only pretend props.
4. Be creative and have fun.

This year, Tony Baloney does not want to wear a costume made from odds and ends.

He does not want to wear one of Big Sister Baloney's hand-me-down costumes, or the same costume as the Bothersome Babies Baloney.

This year, Tony Baloney

wants to stand out in the crowd.

7

The next day, Tony Baloney
uses his savings to buy the costume
he has dreamed of all his life,
or maybe since yesterday.

PARTY
ANTARCTIC
COSTUME

9

At home, everyone is busy
working on their costumes.
Tony Baloney announces,
"I bought a costume
with my own money."

"Be a bumblebee!"
says one Bothersome Baby Baloney.
"Like me!" says the other. "Buzz, buzz!"

★ PARTY ★ ANTARCTIC COSTUME ★

PE ANERS

MARKERS

CREPE PAPER

MAKEUP

Big Sister Baloney gives him *the look*.

"We always *make* our costumes," she says.

"That is part of the fun. You wasted

your money, Tony Baloney."

"You won't say that

when you see it," he says.

Tony Baloney can't wait to show his costume
to his best stuffed animal buddy, Dandelion.

WARNINGS

Tony Baloney loves
his costume so much
that he wears it
a few minutes a day,
or every second all weekend.

"Ahoy, mateys!" he says to
Momma and Poppa Baloney.

"Yo ho ho, ye landlubbers!" he says
to the Bothersome Babies Baloney.

"You are going to ruin your costume,"

says Big Sister Baloney.

"Avast!" says

Tony Baloney.

By Sunday, Tony Baloney's costume
looks a little worn.

Momma Baloney says,
"Tony Baloney, you need to take
better care of your costume
or it will fall apart before
the Halloween parade."

Poppa Baloney says,

"It's important to be responsible

for your things. You don't want

to lose any pieces."

"Aye, aye, captains!"

says Tony Baloney.

The next morning,
Tony Baloney packs his
backpack for school.

"You are not allowed
to wear your costume to school
until the day of the parade,"
warns Big Sister Baloney.
"That's the rule."

"I'm not *wearing* it.

I'm just taking one piece,

to show Bob," says Tony Baloney.

"Good luck with that,"

says Big Sister Baloney.

At school, Tony Baloney shows his best friend Bob

how to brandish his sword.

Tony Baloney does not love trouble . . .

. . . but trouble loves him.

1. No costumes at school until the day of the parade.

2. Nothing pointy or dangerous at school, ever.

3. Use only pretend props.

4. Be creative and have fun.

Mrs. Gamboney is not amused.

"Tony Baloney, you know the rules.

I'm very sorry, but your sword

will have to go into my

Hold-Until-the-End-of-the-Year-Box."

"Too bad about the sword," says Bob.

"At least you still have

all the other cool things."

Tony Baloney perks up.

"But you better guard them

so they will be shipshape

for the parade," warns Bob.

"Count on it, bucko!"

says Tony Baloney.

Costume Catastrophe

Even with all the warnings,

Tony Baloney cannot resist

playing in his costume

now and then,

or all the time.

On the morning of the parade,

Tony Baloney shares his troubles with Dandelion.

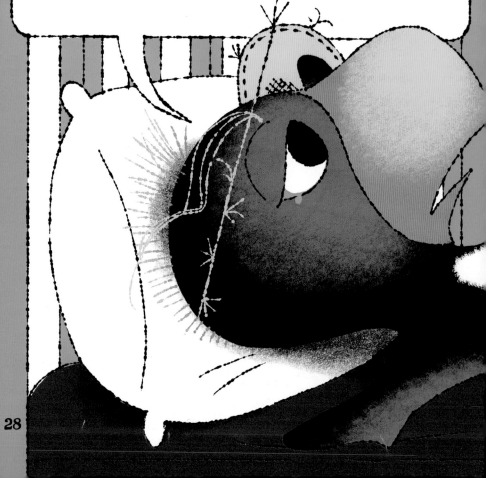

I left the hat on the floor, and the babies used it for a sled. The pants ripped because I was trying to play soccer in them. They were not one bit stretchy! The trash truck ran over the hook because it was left in the street by someone completely irresponsible, or maybe me. I don't know *where* the belt is, maybe with the parrot. I think I left them at the dentist's office.

29

Tony Baloney tells his family what happened.

He waits for Momma Baloney to say,

"You should have been more careful."

He waits for Poppa Baloney to say,

"You should have been more responsible."

He waits for Big Sister Baloney to say,

"I knew you would ruin it."

Instead, Momma Baloney says,

"I think we need a parley.

That's pirate talk for a meeting."

The Baloney family huddles.

Then they get to work.

One Bothersome Baby Baloney

gives Tony Baloney a pair of pirate pants.

The other gives him an eye patch.

Poppa Baloney

quickly makes a hook.

Mama Baloney finds a hat with a plume.

Big Sister Baloney lends him

a pirate blouse and a belt.

What a faithful crew!

Tony Baloney is amazed.

"The only thing missing is a parrot,"

says Big Sister Baloney.

THE PARADE

At the end of the school day,

it is finally time

for the Halloween parade.

Everyone puts on their costumes

and heads outside to the big field.

All the families are waiting.

Brothers and sisters

are invited to join the march.

This year, there are bumblebees

and queens, goblins and ghosts,

football players and fairies,

ninjas and knights, and . . .

. . . a pirate.

This year, Tony Baloney

definitely stands out in the crowd.